Please COME HOME

A book about
divorce
and learning
and growing

© 1985 by Multnomah Press
Printed in Hong Kong
All Rights Reserved.
92 93 - 10 9 8 7 6 5
ISBN 0-88070-138-2
86-106753 CIP

*the story by
Doris Sanford
and pictures by
Graci Evans*

To Christy
and Tim:

very special kids

Jenny sat by the
big apple tree thinking.
She sat there a lot lately.

Something awful had happened.
Mommy said Daddy wasn't
going to live with them anymore.

She **KNEW** they were
having problems.
Why did they pretend
they weren't?

Last night they were yelling
at each other again.
She was afraid Daddy might hit Mommy.
Why couldn't they just say "I'm sorry"
like they told *her* to do when she had a fight?

She felt very mixed up.
And she wondered,
        "Will Mommy go away, too?"

WHAT WILL HAPPEN TO ME?

Mommy said,
  "Daddy wouldn't have left
  if he loved you."

She thought,
  "I'll never speak to my
  Daddy again!"

"I'll be good,
Daddy, if you
come back!
I PROMISE.

*WHY DOESN'T
SOMEBODY
HELP US!"*

Jenny held Teddy tight
and whispered,

"I'm afraid
I'm lonely
I'm sad
I'm unhappy
I'm lost."

And Teddy said in a gentle, quiet voice,

"That's the way ALL children feel when a divorce happens."

And Jenny whispered
again to Teddy,

"Daddy left because I
was too noisy and
didn't clean my room
and bothered him
when he watched
the football game on TV
and I said, 'I hate you,'
once and because
I'm bad!"

And Teddy said,

*"No, that's not
why he left.
You didn't make
him leave by
being bad and
you can't bring
him back by
being good."*

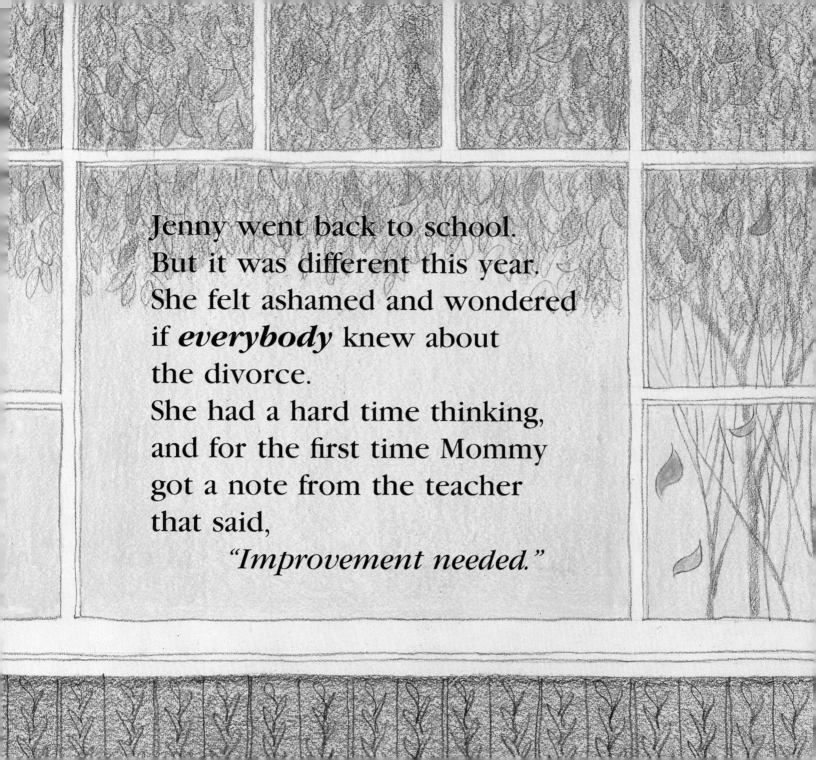

Jenny went back to school.
But it was different this year.
She felt ashamed and wondered
if **everybody** knew about
the divorce.
She had a hard time thinking,
and for the first time Mommy
got a note from the teacher
that said,

"Improvement needed."

On Saturdays she visited Daddy.
It was fun at the park, but
she always cried when
he brought her home.

On her birthday Daddy sent a
package, and she told Mommy,
"I don't want it."
Mommy seemed pleased and
sent it back to Daddy.

Mommy and Daddy fought
on the phone.
Mostly she didn't understand.
It was about court dates, lawyers,
visitation, and dividing furniture.

Jenny's world was turning
upside down and

NOBODY WAS STOPPING IT!

And Jenny squeezed Teddy
and sobbed hard.

"I want to be held
like a small baby
and be
all wrapped up
in a warm blanket."

And Teddy said in his
very tenderest way,

*"I will always be
here for you.
It's okay to cry
and talk about
your feelings."*

And Jenny again whispered to Teddy,

"I want my Mommy and
Daddy to be married again."

And Teddy, who was
especially wise, said:

"We *all* want things
we cannot have
at times.
When this happens
you can change
your mind about
what you want.

You can learn
to be
happy again."

Daddy has a girlfriend now.
He didn't ask Jenny about getting a girlfriend
because her answer would have been **NO**.
Maybe he would marry her and
she would start telling Jenny what to do!

She thought,
        "I already **HAVE** a mother!"

Daddy doesn't always want Jenny on Saturday
because he is busy with his girlfriend.
Jenny wondered why
she didn't have a choice about that.

SOMETIMES she was glad
because Daddy's apartment was so small
and there weren't any kids
to play with anyway.

Mommy has a new job.
When she comes home
she is **"SOOOOO TIRED."**

Then she talks on the phone
to her friend for hours.

She is home. But not really.

The worst thing about not having
very much money anymore is that
Jenny got underwear for Christmas!

UNDERWEAR IS *NOT* A PRESENT!

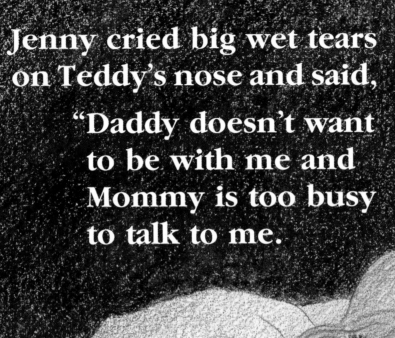

Jenny cried big wet tears
on Teddy's nose and said,

"Daddy doesn't want
to be with me and
Mommy is too busy
to talk to me.

*NOBODY
LOVES ME
ANYMORE."*

**Teddy looked her right
in the eye and said,**

*"Now listen carefully
because this is
very important:*

*YOU ARE LOVEABLE!
YOU ARE PRECIOUS!
YOU ARE SPECIAL!"*

(And Teddy made Jenny repeat it 50 times!)

Jenny told Teddy,

"I don't trust
anybody.

And I
never
ever
will,
either."

And Teddy was sad and said,

*"You won't always
feel that way.*

*Getting over
a divorce
happens a
little bit
at a
time."*

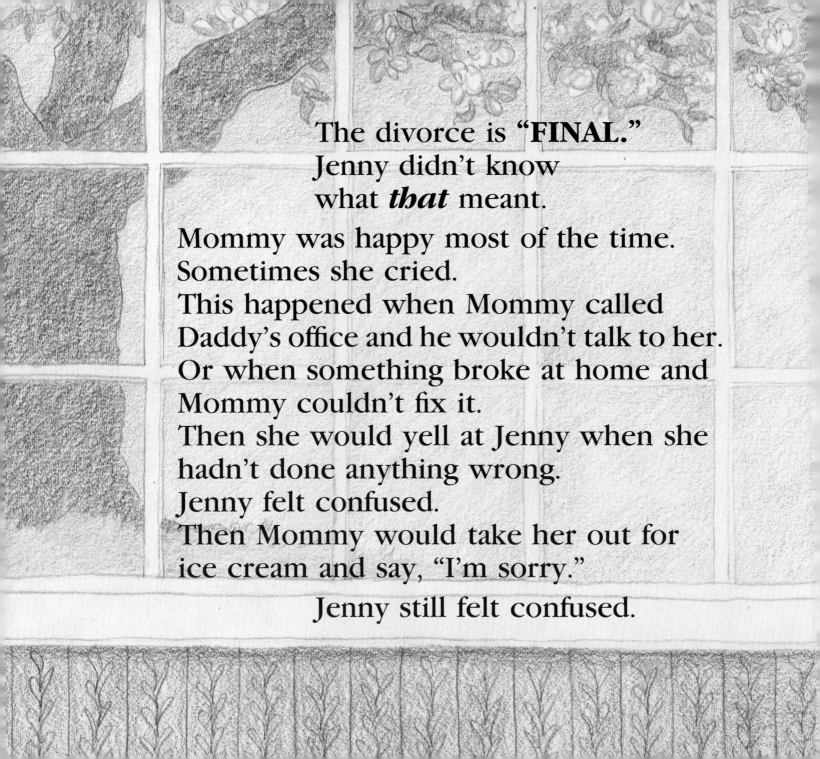

The divorce is **"FINAL."**
Jenny didn't know
what *that* meant.

Mommy was happy most of the time.
Sometimes she cried.
This happened when Mommy called
Daddy's office and he wouldn't talk to her.
Or when something broke at home and
Mommy couldn't fix it.
Then she would yell at Jenny when she
hadn't done anything wrong.
Jenny felt confused.
Then Mommy would take her out for
ice cream and say, "I'm sorry."

Jenny still felt confused.

Jenny usually didn't
like doing grown-up things
that *other* kids
didn't have to do,
like staying by herself
and starting dinner.

But *once in a while*
she felt proud
of herself.

She knew she
was growing up . . .
    not just
    on the outside.

Jenny smiled and told Teddy,

"When I was little
I used to think
that every child
whose parents
were still married
was better off
than me.

Now I know some are
much worse off."

And Teddy said,
"**OH!** *You are* **SO** *smart!*"

Jenny said,

"I used to think
    I'd hurt forever,
But I don't."

And Teddy skipped
a step and said:
    *"I'M SO HAPPY
    I JUST CAN'T
    STAND IT!*

LET'S HUG!"

HOW TO HELP A CHILD WITH DIVORCE:

Dear Friend:

You probably wouldn't be reading this book unless someone you know is divorced. We hope these suggestions will help you better understand the Jennys in your life:

1. For most young children, healing after a divorce takes about one year. If the child is quite upset, professional help may be needed. Time doesn't necessarily heal all wounds.

2. Tell the child how you feel even if you can't fully explain the feeling. Let him see you cry. Say, "I'll talk about it when I'm able."

3. When children are not given facts about the divorce, their imaginations will "fill in the missing pieces." Be gentle with explanations, but tell the truth.

4. Don't weaken the child's relationship with the other parent. Encourage a bond.